D0065232

BAD CATS

CHARLES GHIGNA

ILLUSTRATED BY

DAVID CATROW

Hyperion Books for Children

Text copyright © 1992 by Charles Ghigna
Illustrations copyright © 1992 by David Catrow
All rights reserved.
Printed in the United States of America.
For more information address
Hyperion Books for Children,
114 Fifth Avenue,
New York, New York 10011.

FIRST EDITION
1 3 5 7 9 10 8 6 4 2

Library of Congress Catalog Card Number: 92-52985
ISBN: 1-56282-290-X/1-56282-291-8 (lib. bdg.)

BAD CATS

Cats are mousy,
cats are mean,

Jipp
PEANUT

cats scratch holes
in your new screen.

Tea

Cats are sneaky,
cats are sly,

cats will look you
in the eye.

Cats are lazy,
cats are fat,

cats do nasties
in your hat.

Cats are pious,
cats are rude,

cats stare at you
when you're nude.

TO SEE THE OTHER SIDE OF

CATS,

FLIP THIS BOOK TO START AT THE BEGINNING.

TO SEE THE OTHER SIDE OF

CATS,

FLIP THIS BOOK TO START AT THE BEGINNING.

cats land always
on their feet.

cats are sweet,

Cats are kindly,

cats can clean
their furry suit.

Cats are cuddly,
cats are cute,

cats lie in
the morning sun.

PARCHEEZY

Cats are playful,
cats are fun,

cats are purry
when they dream.

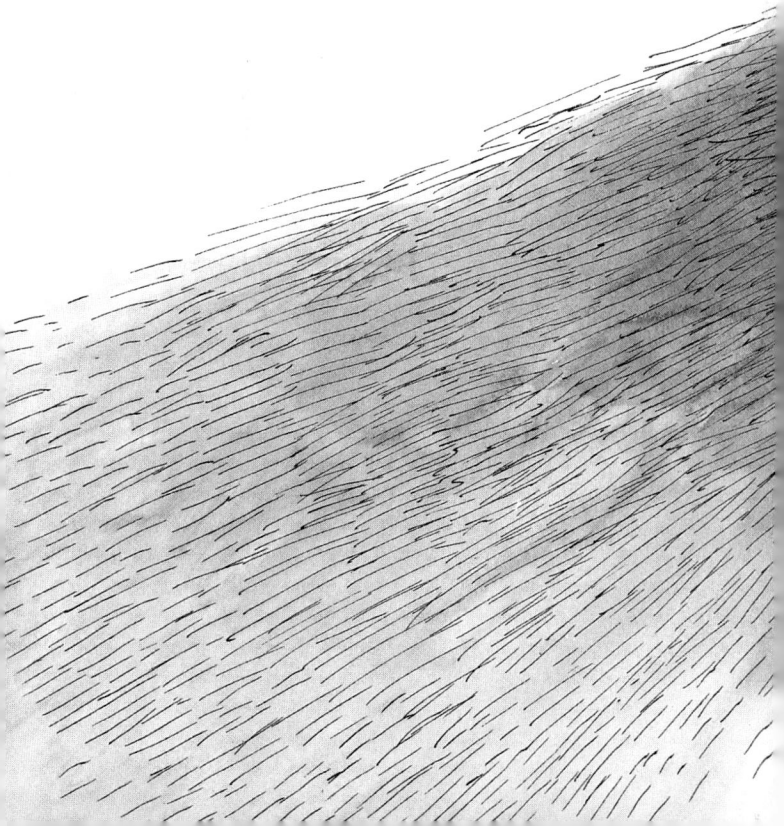

Cats are dainty,
cats are clean,

Good CATS

Text copyright © 1992 by Charles Ghigna
Illustrations copyright © 1992 by David Catrow
All rights reserved.
Printed in the United States of America.
For more information address
Hyperion Books for Children,
114 Fifth Avenue,
New York, New York 10011.

FIRST EDITION
1 3 5 7 9 10 8 6 4 2
Library of Congress Catalog Card Number: 92-52985
ISBN: 1-56282-290-X/1-56282-291-8 (lib. bdg.)

Good CATS

CHARLES GHIGNA

ILLUSTRATED BY
DAVID CATROW

Hyperion Books for Children